A ROOKIE READER®

SHOW AND TELL

By Joanne L. Smith

Illustrated by James Buckley

Prepared under the direction of Robert Hillerich, Ph.D.

 CHILDRENS PRESS®

CHICAGO

For Michael, Paul, and Maggie

Library of Congress Cataloging-in-Publication Data

Smith, Joanne L.
    Show and tell / by Joanne L. Smith ; illustrated by
James Buckley.
        p.   cm. — (A Rookie reader)
    Summary: Billy tends to bring the same thing
every day for show and tell at school, but one day he
brings a surprise.
    ISBN 0-516-02026-9
    1. Toy and movable books—Specimens.
[1. Schools—Fiction. 2. Toy and movable books.]
I. Buckley, James, 1933-   ill. II. Title. III. Series.
PZ7.S6518Sh   1994
[E]—dc20   94-20848
                                               CIP
                                                AC

For show and tell on Monday,

Susie brought her doll

and Billy brought his teddy bear.

For show and tell on Tuesday,

March

Sunday	Monday	Tuesday	Wednesday	Thursday	Friday	Saturday
	1	2	3	4	5	6
7	8	9	10	11	12	13
14	15	16	17	18	19	20
21	22	23	24	25	26	27
28	29	30	31			

Susie brought her ball

9

and Billy brought his teddy bear.

For show and tell on Wednesday,

March

Sunday	Monday	Tuesday	Wednesday	Thursday	Friday	Saturday
	1	2	3	4	5	6
7	8	9	10	11	12	13
14	15	16	17	18	19	20
21	22	23	24	25	26	27
28	29	30	31			

Susie brought her new crayons

and Billy brought his teddy bear.

For show and tell on Thursday,

March

Sunday	Monday	Tuesday	Wednesday	Thursday	Friday	Saturday
	①	②	③	④	5	6
7	8	9	10	11	12	13
14	15	16	17	18	19	20
21	22	23	24	25	26	27
28	29	30	31			

16

Susie brought her favorite book

and Billy brought his teddy bear.

19

For show and tell on Friday,

March

Sunday	Monday	Tuesday	Wednesday	Thursday	Friday	Saturday
	①1	②2	③3	④4	⑤5	6
7	8	9	10	11	12	13
14	15	16	17	18	19	20
21	22	23	24	25	26	27
28	29	30	31			

My Cat

My D

20

Susie brought her drum

and Billy brought his dad.

March
Sunday Monday Tuesday Wednesday Thursday Friday Saturday
1 2 3 4 5 6
7 8 9 10 11 12 13
14 15 16 17 18 19 20
21 22 23 24 25 26 27
28 29 30 31

School is closed on
Saturday and Sunday.

Next week Susie wants to
bring her new red wagon.

27

What will Billy bring?

Pick what you think
Billy will bring
to show and tell!

30

WORD LIST

and	Friday	Susie
ball	her	teddy
bear	his	tell
Billy	is	think
book	Monday	Thursday
bring	new	to
brought	next	Tuesday
closed	on	wagon
crayons	pick	wants
dad	red	Wednesday
doll	Saturday	week
drum	school	what
favorite	show	will
for	Sunday	you

About the Author

Joanne L. Smith lives in Coleman, Michigan with her husband. She has two grown children. She is a kindergarten teacher at Shepherd Elementary School and has taught for over twenty-four years. Joanne loves working with young children.

Some of Joanne's favorite things are sunny days, bright colors, and smiles. Her hobbies are reading, knitting, gardening, and listening to music of all kinds. She enjoys writing stories for her kindergarteners so they can experience her love of reading. *Show and Tell* is her first published work.

About the Artist

James Buckley is a versatile artist who, since graduation from the School of the Art Institute of Chicago, has had a successful career in illustration. His illustrations have appeared in countless children's books. He has worked on many national advertising accounts as well and enjoys working in both the publishing and advertising fields.

Mr. Buckley lives in a suburb of Chicago with his artist wife. Though his schedule is quite demanding, he still finds time to play volleyball three times a week.